Frog and Toad
Storybook Treasury

By Arnold Lobel

HARPER

An Imprint of HarperCollinsPublishers

Contents

Frog and Toad Are Friends   7

SPRING   8

THE STORY   20

A LOST BUTTON   32

A SWIM   44

THE LETTER   57

Frog and Toad Together   69

A LIST   70

THE GARDEN   84

COOKIES   96

DRAGONS AND GIANTS   108

THE DREAM   118

Frog and Toad All Year   131

DOWN THE HILL   132

THE CORNER   146

ICE CREAM   158

THE SURPRISE   170

CHRISTMAS EVE   182

Days With Frog and Toad   193

TOMORROW   194

THE KITE   206

SHIVERS   218

THE HAT   232

ALONE   242

Frog and Toad
Are Friends

Spring

Frog ran up the path
to Toad's house.
He knocked on the front door.
There was no answer.
"Toad, Toad," shouted Frog,
"wake up. It is spring!"
"Blah," said a voice
from inside the house.
"Toad, Toad," cried Frog.

"The sun is shining!

The snow is melting. Wake up!"

"I am not here," said the voice.

9

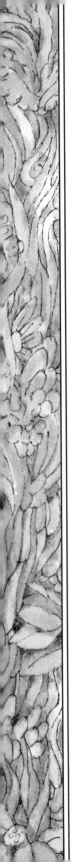

Frog walked into the house.

It was dark.

All the shutters were closed.

"Toad, where are you?" called Frog.

"Go away," said the voice

from a corner of the room.

Toad was lying in bed.

He had pulled all the covers
over his head.

Frog pushed Toad out of bed.

He pushed him out of the house
and onto the front porch.

Toad blinked in the bright sun.

"Help!" said Toad.

"I cannot see anything."

"Don't be silly," said Frog.

"What you see

is the clear warm light of April.

And it means

that we can begin

a whole new year together, Toad.

Think of it," said Frog.

"We will skip through the meadows

and run through the woods

and swim in the river.

In the evenings we will sit

right here on this front porch

and count the stars."

"You can count them, Frog,"
said Toad. "I will be too tired.
I am going back to bed."

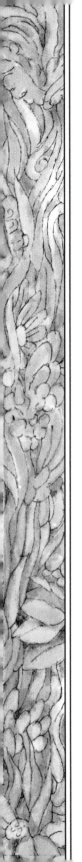

Toad went back into the house.

He got into the bed

and pulled the covers

over his head again.

"But, Toad," cried Frog,

"you will miss all the fun!"

"Listen, Frog," said Toad.

"How long have I been asleep?"

"You have been asleep
since November," said Frog.
"Well then," said Toad,
"a little more sleep
will not hurt me.
Come back again and wake me up
at about half past May.
Good night, Frog."

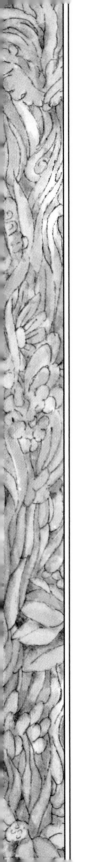

"But, Toad," said Frog,

"I will be lonely until then."

Toad did not answer.

He had fallen asleep.

Frog looked at Toad's calendar.

The November page was still on top.

Frog tore off the November page.

He tore off the December page.

And the January page,

the February page,

and the March page.

He came to the April page.

Frog tore off the April page too.

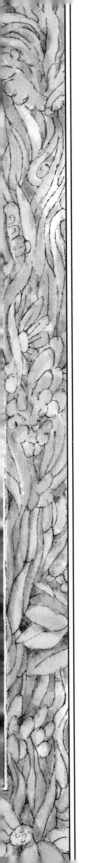

Then Frog ran back to Toad's bed.

"Toad, Toad, wake up.

It is May now."

"What?" said Toad.

"Can it be May so soon?"

"Yes," said Frog.

"Look at your calendar."

Toad looked at the calendar.

The May page was on top.

"Why, it *is* May!" said Toad
as he climbed out of bed.
Then he and Frog
ran outside
to see how the world
was looking in the spring.

The Story

One day in summer
Frog was not feeling well.
Toad said, "Frog,
you are looking quite green."
"But I always look green,"
said Frog. "I am a frog."
"Today you look very green
even for a frog," said Toad.
"Get into my bed and rest."

Toad made Frog a cup of hot tea.

Frog drank the tea, and then he said,

"Tell me a story while I am resting."

21

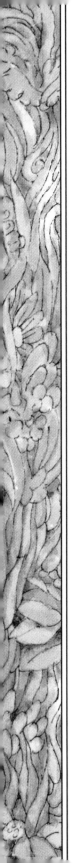

"All right," said Toad.

"Let me think of a story to tell you."

Toad thought and thought.

But he could not think of a story

to tell Frog.

"I will go out on the front porch
and walk up and down," said Toad.
"Perhaps that will help me
to think of a story."
Toad walked up and down
on the porch for a long time.
But he could not think of a story
to tell Frog.

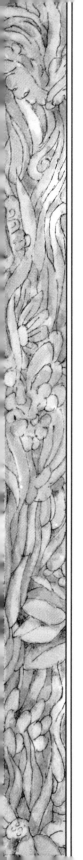

Then Toad went into the house
and stood on his head.
"Why are you standing
on your head?" asked Frog.
"I hope that if I stand on my head,
it will help me
to think of a story," said Toad.

Toad stood on his head

for a long time.

But he could not think

of a story to tell Frog.

Then Toad poured a glass of water
over his head.

"Why are you pouring water
over your head?" asked Frog.

"I hope that if I pour water
over my head,
it will help me to think
of a story," said Toad.

Toad poured many glasses of water
over his head.

But he could not think
of a story to tell Frog.

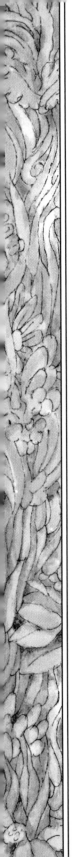

Then Toad began
to bang his head
against the wall.

"Why are you banging your head
against the wall?" asked Frog.

"I hope that if I bang my head
against the wall hard enough,
it will help me to think of a story,"
said Toad.

"I am feeling much better now, Toad,"
said Frog. "I do not think
I need a story anymore."
"Then you get out of bed
and let me get into it," said Toad,
"because now I feel terrible."
Frog said, "Would you like me
to tell you a story, Toad?"
"Yes," said Toad, "if you know one."

"Once upon a time," said Frog,

"there were two good friends,

a frog and a toad.

The frog was not feeling well.

He asked his friend the toad

to tell him a story.

The toad could not think of a story.

He walked up and down on the porch,

but he could not think of a story.

He stood on his head,

but he could not think of a story.

He poured water over his head,

but he could not think of a story.

He banged his head against the wall,

but he still could not think

of a story.

Then the toad did not feel so well,

and the frog was feeling better.

So the toad went to bed

and the frog got up

and told him a story.

The end.

How was that,

Toad?" said Frog.

But Toad did not answer.

He had fallen asleep.

A Lost Button

Toad and Frog

went for a long walk.

They walked across

a large meadow.

They walked in the woods.

They walked along the river.

At last they went back home

to Toad's house.

"Oh, drat," said Toad.

"Not only do my feet hurt,

but I have lost

one of the buttons on my jacket."

"Don't worry," said Frog.

"We will go back

to all the places where we walked.

We will soon find your button."

They walked back to the large meadow.

They began to look for the button

in the tall grass.

"Here is your button!" cried Frog.

"That is not my button," said Toad.

"That button is black.

My button was white."

Toad put the black button

in his pocket.

A sparrow flew down.

"Excuse me," said the sparrow.

"Did you lose a button? I found one."

"That is not my button," said Toad.

"That button has two holes.

My button had four holes."

Toad put the button with two holes

in his pocket.

They went back to the woods
and looked on the dark paths.

"Here is your button," said Frog.

"That is not my button," cried Toad.

"That button is small.

My button was big."

Toad put the small button
in his pocket.

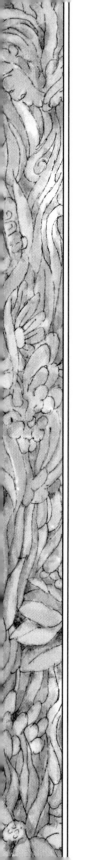

A raccoon came out from behind a tree.

"I heard that you were looking

for a button," he said.

"Here is one that I just found."

"That is not my button!" wailed Toad.

"That button is square.

My button was round."

Toad put the square button

in his pocket.

Frog and Toad went back to the river.

They looked for the button

in the mud.

"Here is your button," said Frog.

"That is not my button!" shouted Toad.

"That button is thin.

My button was thick."

Toad put the thin button
in his pocket. He was very angry.
He jumped up and down
and screamed,
"The whole world
is covered with buttons,
and not one of them is mine!"

Toad ran home and slammed the door.

There, on the floor,

he saw his white, four-holed,

big, round, thick button.

"Oh," said Toad.

"It was here all the time.

What a lot of trouble

I have made for Frog."

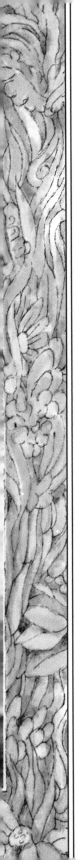

Toad took all of the buttons

out of his pocket.

He took his sewing box

down from the shelf.

Toad sewed the buttons

all over his jacket.

The next day Toad gave

his jacket to Frog.

Frog thought that it was beautiful.

He put it on and jumped for joy.

None of the buttons fell off.

Toad had sewed them on very well.

A Swim

Toad and Frog

went down to the river.

"What a day for a swim," said Frog.

"Yes," said Toad.

"I will go behind these rocks

and put on my bathing suit."

"I don't wear a bathing suit,"

said Frog.

"Well, I do," said Toad.

"After I put on my bathing suit,
you must not look at me
until I get into the water."

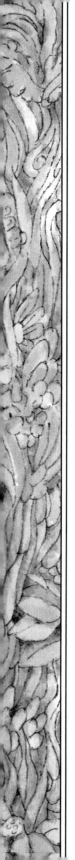

"Why not?"

asked Frog.

"Because I look funny

in my bathing suit.

That is why," said Toad.

Frog closed his eyes when Toad

came out from behind the rocks.

Toad was wearing his bathing suit.

"Don't peek," he said.

Frog and Toad jumped

into the water.

They swam all afternoon.

Frog swam fast

and made big splashes.

Toad swam slowly

and made smaller splashes.

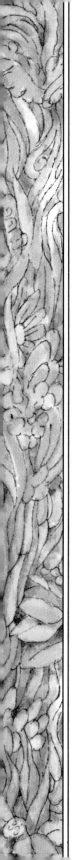

A turtle came along the riverbank.

"Frog, tell that turtle

to go away," said Toad.

"I do not want him to see me

in my bathing suit

when I come out of the river."

Frog swam over to the turtle.

"Turtle," said Frog,

"you will have to go away."

"Why should I?" asked the turtle.

"Because Toad thinks that

he looks funny in his bathing suit,

and he does not want you to see him,"

said Frog.

Some lizards were sitting nearby.

"Does Toad really look funny

in his bathing suit?" they asked.

A snake crawled out of the grass.

"If Toad looks funny

in his bathing suit," said the snake,

"then I, for one, want to see him."

"We want to see him too,"
said two dragonflies.

"Me too," said a field mouse.
"I have not seen anything funny
in a long time."

Frog swam back to Toad.

"I am sorry, Toad," he said. "Everyone

wants to see how you will look."

"Then I will stay right here

until they go away," said Toad.

The turtle and the lizards

and the snake and the dragonflies

and the field mouse

all sat on the riverbank.

They waited for Toad to come

out of the water.

"Please," cried Frog, "please go away!"

But no one went away.

Toad was getting colder and colder.

He was beginning to shiver and sneeze.

"I will have to come out of the water,"

said Toad. "I am catching a cold."

Toad climbed
out of the river.
The water dripped
out of his bathing suit
and down onto his feet.

The turtle laughed.

The lizards laughed.

The snake laughed.

The field mouse laughed,

and Frog laughed.

"What are you laughing at, Frog?"
said Toad.

"I am laughing at you, Toad,"
said Frog,

"because you *do* look funny
in your bathing suit."

"Of course I do," said Toad.
Then he picked up his clothes
and went home.

The Letter

Toad was sitting on his front porch.

Frog came along and said,

"What is the matter, Toad?

You are looking sad."

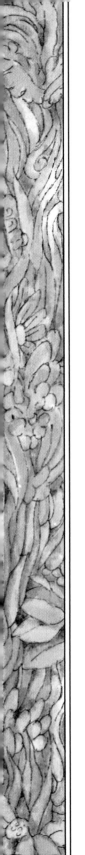

"Yes," said Toad.

"This is my sad time of day.

It is the time

when I wait for the mail to come.

It always makes me very unhappy."

"Why is that?" asked Frog.

"Because I never get any mail,"

said Toad.

"Not ever?" asked Frog.

"No, never," said Toad.

"No one has ever sent me a letter.

Every day my mailbox is empty.

That is why waiting for the mail

is a sad time for me."

Frog and Toad sat on the porch,

feeling sad together.

Then Frog said,

"I have to go home now, Toad.

There is something that I must do."

Frog hurried home.

He found a pencil

and a piece of paper.

He wrote on the paper.

He put the paper in an envelope.

On the envelope he wrote

"A LETTER FOR TOAD."

Frog ran out of his house.

He saw a snail that he knew.

"Snail," said Frog, "please take

this letter to Toad's house

and put it in his mailbox."

"Sure," said the snail. "Right away."

Then Frog ran back to Toad's house.

Toad was in bed, taking a nap.

"Toad," said Frog,

"I think you should get up

and wait for the mail some more."

"No," said Toad,

"I am tired of waiting for the mail."

Frog looked out of the window
at Toad's mailbox.

The snail was not there yet.

"Toad," said Frog, "you never know
when someone may send you a letter."

"No, no," said Toad. "I do not think
anyone will ever send me a letter."

Frog looked out of the window.

The snail was not there yet.

"But, Toad," said Frog,

"someone may send you a letter today."

"Don't be silly," said Toad.

"No one has ever sent me

a letter before, and no one

will send me a letter today."

Frog looked out of the window.

The snail was still not there.

"Frog, why do you keep looking

out of the window?" asked Toad.

"Because now I am waiting

for the mail," said Frog.

"But there will not be any," said Toad.

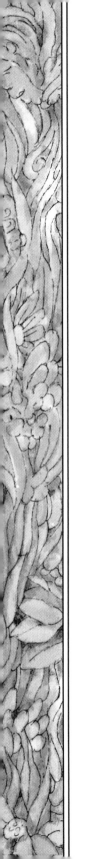

"Oh, yes there will," said Frog,

"because I have sent you a letter."

"You have?" said Toad.

"What did you write in the letter?"

Frog said, "I wrote

'Dear Toad, I am glad

that you are my best friend.

Your best friend, Frog.'"

66

"Oh," said Toad,

"that makes a very good letter."

Then Frog and Toad went out

onto the front porch

to wait for the mail.

They sat there,

feeling happy together.

Frog and Toad waited a long time.

Four days later

the snail got to Toad's house

and gave him the letter from Frog.

Toad was very pleased to have it.

Frog and Toad Together

A List

One morning Toad sat in bed.

"I have many things to do," he said.

"I will write them

all down on a list

so that I can remember them."

Toad wrote on a piece of paper:

A List of things to do today

Then he wrote:

Wake up

"I have done that," said Toad,

and he crossed out:

Then Toad wrote other things
on the paper.

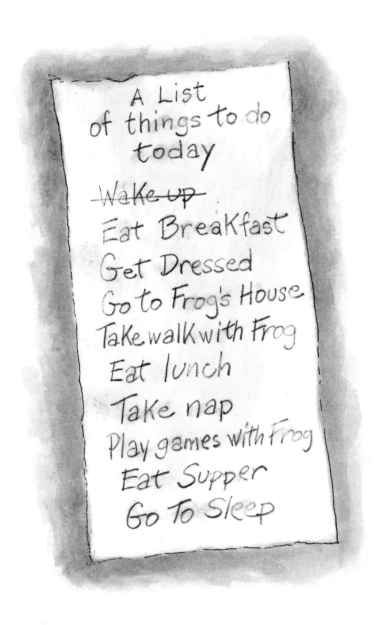

A List
of things to do
today

~~Wake up~~
Eat Breakfast
Get Dressed
Go to Frog's House
Take walk with Frog
Eat lunch
Take nap
Play games with Frog
Eat Supper
Go To Sleep

"There," said Toad.

"Now my day

is all written down."

He got out of bed

and had something to eat.

Then Toad crossed out:

~~Eat Breakfast~~

Toad took his clothes

out of the closet

and put them on.

Then he crossed out:

~~Get Dressed~~

Toad put the list in his pocket.

He opened the door

and walked out into the morning.

Soon Toad was at Frog's front door.

He took the list from his pocket

and crossed out:

~~Go to Frog's House~~

Toad knocked at the door.

"Hello," said Frog.

"Look at my list

of things to do,"

said Toad.

"Oh," said Frog,

"that is very nice."

Toad said, "My list tells me

that we will go

for a walk."

"All right," said Frog.

"I am ready."

Frog and Toad

went on a long walk.

Then Toad took the list

from his pocket again.

He crossed out:

~~Take walk with Frog~~

Just then there was a strong wind.

It blew the list

out of Toad's hand.

The list blew high up

into the air.

"Help!" cried Toad.

"My list is blowing away.

What will I do without my list?"

"Hurry!" said Frog.

"We will run and catch it."

"No!" shouted Toad.

"I cannot do that."

"Why not?" asked Frog.

"Because," wailed Toad,

"running after my list

is not one of the things

that I wrote

on my list of things to do!"

Frog ran after the list.

He ran over hills and swamps,

but the list blew on and on.

At last Frog came back to Toad.

"I am sorry," gasped Frog,

"but I could not catch

your list."

"Blah," said Toad.

"I cannot remember any of the things
that were on my list of things to do.
I will just have to sit here
and do nothing," said Toad.
Toad sat and did nothing.
Frog sat with him.

After a long time Frog said,
"Toad, it is getting dark.
We should be going to sleep now."

"Go to sleep!" shouted Toad.

"That was the last thing on my list!"

Toad wrote on the ground

with a stick: Go to sleep

Then he crossed out:

~~Go to sleep~~

"There," said Toad.

"Now my day

is all crossed out!"

"I am glad,"

said Frog.

Then Frog and Toad

went right to sleep.

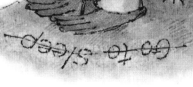

The Garden

Frog was in his garden.

Toad came walking by.

"What a fine garden

you have, Frog," he said.

"Yes," said Frog. "It is very nice,

but it was hard work."

"I wish I had a garden," said Toad.

"Here are some flower seeds.

Plant them in the ground," said Frog,

"and soon you will have a garden."

"How soon?" asked Toad.

"Quite soon," said Frog.

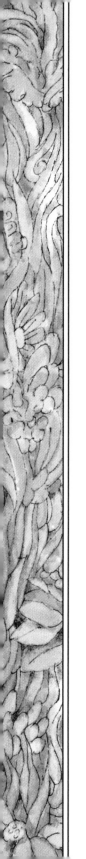

Toad ran home.

He planted the flower seeds.

"Now seeds," said Toad,

"start growing."

Toad walked up and down

a few times.

The seeds did not start to grow.

Toad put his head

close to the ground

and said loudly,

"Now seeds, start growing!"

Toad looked at the ground again.

The seeds did not start to grow.

Toad put his head

very close to the ground and shouted,

"NOW SEEDS, START GROWING!"

Frog came running up the path.

"What is all this noise?" he asked.

"My seeds will not grow," said Toad.

"You are shouting too much,"

said Frog. "These poor seeds

are afraid to grow."

"My seeds are afraid to grow?"

asked Toad.

"Of course," said Frog.

"Leave them alone for a few days.

Let the sun shine on them,

let the rain fall on them.

Soon your seeds will start to grow."

That night

Toad looked out of his window.

"Drat!" said Toad.

"My seeds have not

started to grow.

They must be afraid of the dark."

Toad went out to his garden

with some candles.

"I will read the seeds a story,"

said Toad.

"Then they will not be afraid."

Toad read a long story

to his seeds.

All the next day
Toad sang songs
to his seeds.

And all the next day
Toad read poems
to his seeds.

And all the next day
Toad played music
for his seeds.

Toad looked at the ground.

The seeds still did not

start to grow.

"What shall I do?" cried Toad.

"These must be

the most frightened seeds

in the whole world!"

Then Toad felt very tired

and he fell asleep.

"Toad, Toad, wake up," said Frog.

"Look at your garden!"

Toad looked at his garden.

Little green plants were coming up
out of the ground.

"At last," shouted Toad,
"my seeds have stopped
being afraid to grow!"
"And now you will have
a nice garden too," said Frog.
"Yes," said Toad,
"but you were right, Frog.
It was very hard work."

Cookies

Toad baked some cookies.

"These cookies smell very good,"

said Toad.

He ate one.

"And they taste even better," he said.

Toad ran to Frog's house.

"Frog, Frog," cried Toad,

"taste these cookies

that I have made."

Frog ate one of the cookies.

"These are the best cookies

I have ever eaten!" said Frog.

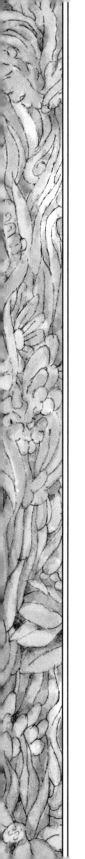

Frog and Toad ate many cookies,
one after another.

"You know, Toad," said Frog,
with his mouth full,
"I think we should stop eating.
We will soon be sick."

"You are right," said Toad.

"Let us eat one last cookie,

and then we will stop."

Frog and Toad ate

one last cookie.

There were many cookies

left in the bowl.

"Frog," said Toad,

"let us eat one very last cookie,

and then we will stop."

Frog and Toad

ate one very last cookie.

"We must stop eating!" cried Toad
as he ate another.
"Yes," said Frog,
reaching for a cookie,
"we need will power."
"What is will power?" asked Toad.

"Will power is trying hard
not to do something
that you really want to do,"
said Frog.

"You mean like trying *not*
to eat all of these cookies?"
asked Toad.

"Right," said Frog.

Frog put the cookies in a box.

"There," he said.

"Now we will not eat
any more cookies."

"But we can open the box,"
said Toad.

"That is true," said Frog.

Frog tied some string

around the box.

"There," he said.

"Now we will not eat

any more cookies."

"But we can cut the string

and open the box," said Toad.

"That is true," said Frog.

Frog got a ladder.

He put the box up on a high shelf.

"There," said Frog.

"Now we will not eat

any more cookies."

"But we can climb the ladder

and take the box

down from the shelf

and cut the string

and open the box,"

said Toad.

"That is true," said Frog.

Frog climbed the ladder

and took the box

down from the shelf.

He cut the string

and opened the box.

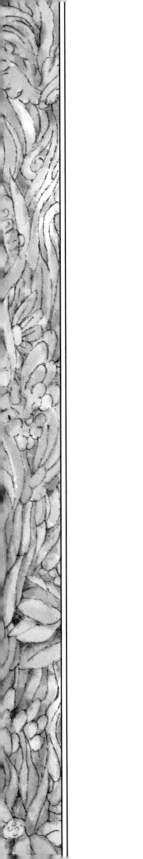

Frog took the box outside.

He shouted in a loud voice,

"HEY BIRDS,

HERE ARE COOKIES!"

Birds came from everywhere.

They picked up all the cookies

in their beaks and flew away.

"Now we have no more cookies to eat,"

said Toad sadly.

"Not even one."

"Yes," said Frog,

"but we have lots and lots

of will power."

"You may keep it all, Frog,"

said Toad.

"I am going home now

to bake a cake."

Dragons and Giants

Frog and Toad

were reading a book together.

"The people in this book

are brave," said Toad.

"They fight dragons and giants,

and they are never afraid."

"I wonder if we are brave,"

said Frog.

Frog and Toad looked into a mirror.

"We look brave," said Frog.

"Yes, but are we?"

asked Toad.

Frog and Toad went outside.

"We can try to climb this mountain,"
said Frog. "That should tell us
if we are brave."

Frog went leaping over rocks,
and Toad came puffing up
behind him.

They came to a dark cave.

A big snake came out of the cave.

"Hello lunch," said the snake

when he saw Frog and Toad.

He opened his wide mouth.

Frog and Toad jumped away.

Toad was shaking.

"I am not afraid!" he cried.

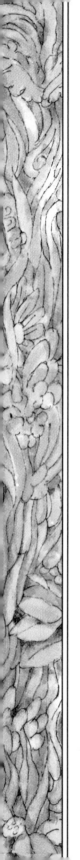

They climbed higher,

and they heard a loud noise.

Many large stones

were rolling down the mountain.

"It's an avalanche!" cried Toad.

Frog and Toad jumped away.

Frog was trembling.

"I am not afraid!" he shouted.

They came to the top

of the mountain.

The shadow of a hawk

fell over them.

Frog and Toad

jumped under a rock.

The hawk flew away.

"We are not afraid!"

screamed Frog and Toad

at the same time.

Then they ran down the mountain

very fast.

They ran past the place

where they saw the avalanche.

They ran past the place

where they saw the snake.

They ran all the way

to Toad's house.

"Frog, I am glad to have

a brave friend like you," said Toad.

He jumped into the bed

and pulled the covers

over his head.

"And I am happy to know

a brave person like you, Toad,"

said Frog.

He jumped into the closet

and shut the door.

Toad stayed in the bed,

and Frog stayed in the closet.

They stayed there

for a long time,

just feeling very brave together.

The Dream

Toad was asleep,

and he was having a dream.

He was on a stage,

and he was wearing

a costume.

Toad looked out

into the dark.

Frog was sitting

in the theater.

A strange voice from far away said,

"PRESENTING THE GREATEST TOAD

IN ALL THE WORLD!"

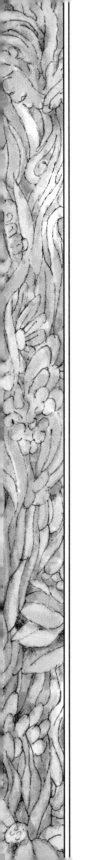

Toad took a deep bow.

Frog looked smaller
as he shouted,
"Hooray for Toad!"
"TOAD WILL NOW
PLAY THE PIANO VERY WELL,"
said the strange voice.

Toad played the piano,

and he did not miss a note.

"Frog," cried Toad,

"can you play the piano like this?"

"No," said Frog.

It seemed to Toad

that Frog looked even smaller.

"TOAD WILL NOW WALK

ON A HIGH WIRE,

AND HE WILL NOT FALL DOWN,"

said the voice.

Toad walked on the high wire.

"Frog," cried Toad,

"can you do tricks like this?"

"No," peeped Frog,

who looked very, very small.

"TOAD WILL NOW DANCE,

AND HE WILL BE WONDERFUL,"

said the voice.

"Frog, can you be as wonderful

as this?" said Toad

as he danced all over the stage.

There was no answer.

Toad looked out into the theater.

Frog was so small

that he could not be seen or heard.

"Frog," said Toad,

"where are you?"

There was still no answer.

"Frog, what have I done?"

cried Toad.

Then the voice said,

"THE GREATEST TOAD WILL NOW . . ."

"Shut up!" screamed Toad.

"Frog, Frog, where have you gone?"

Toad was spinning in the dark.

"Come back, Frog," he shouted.

"I will be lonely!"

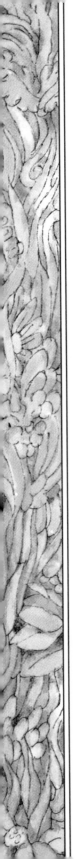

"I am right here," said Frog.

Frog was standing near Toad's bed.

"Wake up, Toad," he said.

"Frog, is that really you?" said Toad.

"Of course it is me," said Frog.

"And are you

your own right size?" asked Toad.

"Yes, I think so," said Frog.

Toad looked at the sunshine

coming through the window.

"Frog," he said,

"I am so glad

that you came over."

"I always do," said Frog.

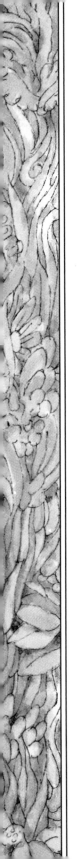

Then Frog and Toad

ate a big breakfast.

And after that

they spent a fine, long day together.

Frog and Toad
All Year

Down the Hill

Frog knocked at Toad's door.

"Toad, wake up," he cried.

"Come out and see

how wonderful the winter is!"

"I will not," said Toad.

"I am in my warm bed."

"Winter is beautiful,"

said Frog.

"Come out and have fun."

"Blah," said Toad.

"I do not have
any winter clothes."

133

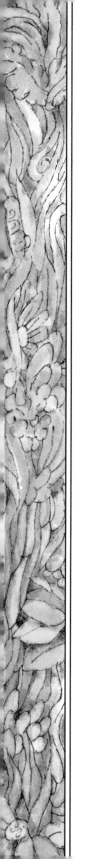

Frog came into the house.

"I have brought you

some things to wear," he said.

Frog pushed a coat

down over the top of Toad.

Frog pulled snowpants

up over the bottom of Toad.

He put a hat and scarf

on Toad's head.

"Help!" cried Toad.

"My best friend

is trying to kill me!"

"I am only getting you ready

for winter," said Frog.

Frog and Toad went outside.

They tramped through the snow.

"We will ride

down this big hill

on my sled," said Frog.

"Not me," said Toad.

"Do not be afraid," said Frog.

"I will be with you

on the sled.

It will be a fine, fast ride.

Toad, you sit in front.

I will sit right behind you."

The sled began to move

down the hill.

"Here we go!"

said Frog.

There was a bump.

Frog fell off the sled.

Toad rushed past trees and rocks.

"Frog, I am glad

that you are here," said Toad.

Toad leaped over

a snowbank.

"I could not steer the sled

without you, Frog," he said.

"You are right. Winter is fun!"

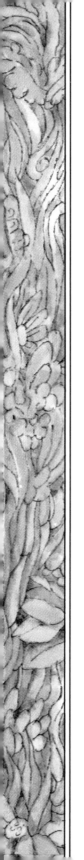

A crow flew nearby.

"Hello, Crow," shouted Toad.

"Look at Frog and me.

We can ride a sled

better than anybody

in the world!"

"But Toad," said the crow,

"you are alone on the sled."

Toad looked around.

He saw that Frog was not there.

"I AM ALL ALONE!"

screamed Toad.

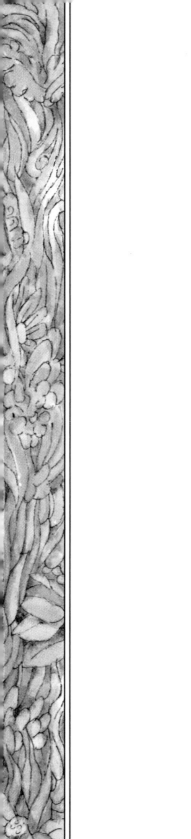

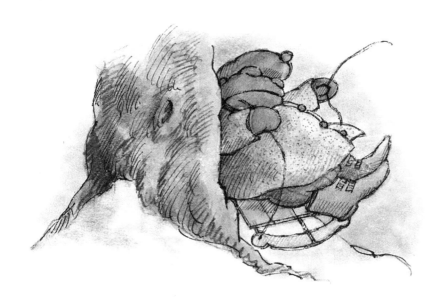

Bang!

The sled hit a tree.

Thud!

The sled hit a rock.

Plop!

The sled dived

into the snow.

143

Frog came running down the hill.

He pulled Toad out of the snow.

"I saw everything," said Frog.

"You did very well

by yourself."

"I did not," said Toad.

"But there is one thing

that I can do

all by myself."

"What is that?" asked Frog.

"I can go home," said Toad.

"Winter may be beautiful,

but bed is much better."

The Corner

Frog and Toad

were caught in the rain.

They ran to Frog's house.

"I am all wet," said Toad.

"The day is spoiled."

"Have some tea and cake,"

said Frog. "The rain will stop.

If you stand near the stove,

your clothes will soon be dry.

I will tell you a story

while we are waiting," said Frog.

"Oh good," said Toad.

"When I was small,

not much bigger

than a pollywog," said Frog,

"my father said to me,

'Son, this is a cold, gray day

but spring

is just around the corner.'

I wanted spring to come.

I went out

to find that corner.

I walked down a path in the woods

until I came to a corner.

I went around the corner

to see if spring

was on the other side."

"And was it?" asked Toad.

"No," said Frog.

"There was only a pine tree,

three pebbles

and some dry grass.

I walked

in the meadow.

Soon I came to

another corner.

I went around the corner

to see if spring was there."

"Did you find it?" asked Toad.

"No," said Frog.

"There was only

an old worm

asleep on a

tree stump."

"I walked along the river
until I came to
another corner.
I went around the corner
to look for spring."

"Was it there?" asked Toad.

"No," said Frog.
"There was only
some wet mud
and a lizard who was chasing
his tail."
"You must have been tired,"
said Toad.
"I was tired," said Frog,
"and it started
to rain."

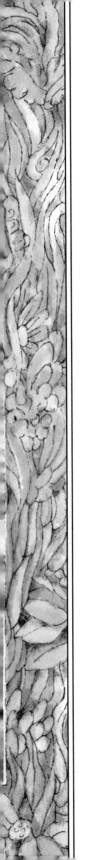

"I went back home.

When I got there," said Frog,

"I found another corner.

It was the corner of my house."

"Did you go around it?"

asked Toad.

"I went around that corner, too,"

said Frog.

"What did you see?"

asked Toad.

"I saw the sun coming out,"
said Frog. "I saw the birds
sitting and singing in the tree.
I saw my mother and father
working in their garden.
I saw flowers in the garden."

"You found it!" cried Toad.

"Yes," said Frog.

"I was very happy.

I had found the corner

that spring was just around."

"Look, Frog," said Toad.

"You were right.

The rain has stopped."

Frog and Toad hurried outside.

They ran around the corner
of Frog's house
to make sure
that spring had come again.

Ice Cream

One hot summer day

Frog and Toad sat by the pond.

"I wish we had some

sweet, cold ice cream," said Frog.

"What a good idea," said Toad.

"Wait right here, Frog.

I will be back soon."

Toad went to the store.

He bought two big ice-cream cones.

Toad licked one of the cones.

"Frog likes chocolate best,"

said Toad, "and so do I."

Toad walked along the path.

A large, soft drop

of chocolate ice cream

slipped down his arm.

"This ice cream

is melting in the sun,"

said Toad.

Toad walked faster.

Many drops

of melting ice cream

flew through the air.

They fell down on Toad's head.

"I must hurry back

to Frog!" he cried.

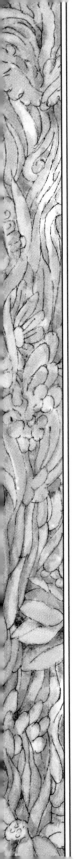

More and more
of the ice cream
was melting.
It dripped down
on Toad's jacket.
It splattered
on his pants
and on his feet.
"Where is the path?"
cried Toad.
"I cannot see!"

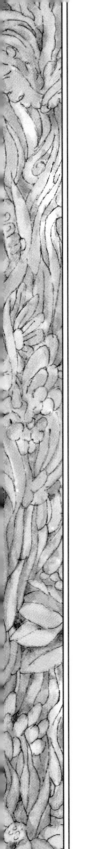

Frog sat by the pond
waiting for Toad.
A mouse ran by.

"I just saw something awful!"
cried the mouse.
"It was big and brown!"

"Something covered

with sticks and leaves is moving

this way!" cried a squirrel.

"Here comes a thing with horns!"

shouted a rabbit.

"Run for your life!"

"What can it be?" asked Frog.

Frog hid behind a rock.

He saw the thing coming.

It was big and brown.

It was covered

with sticks and leaves.

It had two horns.

"Frog," cried the thing.

"Where are you?"

"Good heavens!"

said Frog.

"That thing is Toad!"

Toad fell into the pond.

He sank to the bottom

and came up again.

"Drat," said Toad.

"All of our sweet, cold ice cream

has washed away."

"Never mind," said Frog.

"I know what we can do."

Frog and Toad quickly ran back

to the store.

Then they sat in the shade

of a large tree

and ate

their chocolate

ice-cream cones

together.

The Surprise

It was October.

The leaves had fallen off

the trees.

They were lying on the ground.

"I will go to Toad's house,"

said Frog.

"I will rake all of the leaves

that have fallen on his lawn.

Toad will be surprised."

Frog took a rake

out of the

garden shed.

Toad looked out of his window.

"These messy leaves

have covered everything," said Toad.

He took a rake out of the closet.

"I will run over to Frog's house.

I will rake all of his leaves.

Frog will be very pleased."

Frog ran through the woods

so that Toad would not see him.

Toad ran through the high grass

so that Frog would not see him.

Frog came to Toad's house.

He looked in the window.

"Good," said Frog.

"Toad is out.

He will never know

who raked his leaves."

Toad got to Frog's house.

He looked in the window.

"Good," said Toad.

"Frog is not home.

He will never guess

who raked his leaves."

Frog worked hard.

He raked the leaves into a pile.

Soon Toad's lawn was clean.

Frog picked up his rake

and started home.

Toad pushed and pulled on the rake.

He raked the leaves into a pile.

Soon there was not a single leaf

in Frog's front yard.

Toad took his rake

and started home.

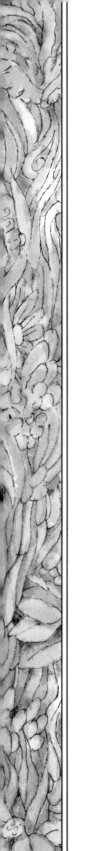

A wind came.

It blew across the land.

The pile of leaves

that Frog had raked for Toad

blew everywhere.

The pile of leaves

that Toad had raked for Frog

blew everywhere.

When Frog got home,

he said, "Tomorrow I will

clean up the leaves

that are all over my own lawn.

How surprised Toad must be!"

When Toad got home,

he said, "Tomorrow I will

get to work and rake

all of my own leaves.

How surprised Frog must be!"

That night
Frog and Toad
were both happy
when they each
turned out the light
and went to bed.

Christmas Eve

On Christmas Eve

Toad cooked a big dinner.

He decorated the tree.

"Frog is late," said Toad.

Toad looked at his clock.

He remembered it was broken.

The hands of the clock did not move.

Toad opened the front door.

He looked out into the night.

Frog was not there.

"I am worried,"

said Toad.

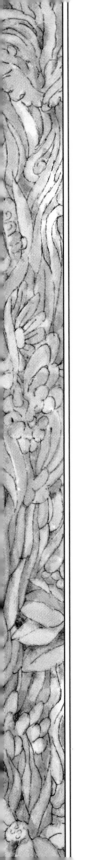

"What if something terrible
has happened?" said Toad.
"What if Frog has fallen
into a deep hole
and cannot get out?
I will never see him again!"

Toad opened the door once more.

Frog was not on the path.

"What if Frog is lost

in the woods?"

said Toad.

"What if

he is cold

and wet

and hungry?"

"What if Frog is being chased
by a big animal
with many sharp teeth?
What if he is being eaten up?"
cried Toad.
"My friend and I
will never have
another Christmas together!"

Toad found some rope in the cellar.

"I will pull Frog out of the hole

with this," said Toad.

Toad found a lantern in the attic.

"Frog will see this light.

I will show him the way

out of the woods," said Toad.

Toad found a frying pan

in the kitchen.

"I will hit that big animal

with this," said Toad.

"All of his teeth

will fall out.

Frog, do not worry," cried Toad.

"I am coming to help you!"

Toad ran out

of his house.

189

There was Frog.

"Hello, Toad," he said.

"I am very sorry to be late.

I was wrapping your present."

"You are not at the bottom

of a hole?" asked Toad.

"No," said Frog.

"You are not lost

in the woods?" asked Toad.

"No," said Frog.

"You are not being eaten

by a big animal?"

asked Toad.

"No," said Frog. "Not at all."

"Oh, Frog," said Toad,

"I am so glad to be

spending Christmas with you."

Toad opened his present from Frog.

It was a beautiful new clock.

The two friends sat by the fire.

The hands of the clock

moved to show the hours

of a merry Christmas Eve.

Days With
Frog and Toad

Tomorrow

Toad woke up.

"Drat!" he said.

"This house is a mess.

I have so much work to do."

Frog looked through the window.

"Toad, you are right,"

said Frog. "It is a mess."

Toad pulled the covers

over his head.

"I will do it tomorrow,"

said Toad.

"Today I will take life easy."

Frog came into the house.

"Toad," said Frog,

"your pants and jacket

are lying on the floor."

"Tomorrow," said Toad

from under the covers.

"Your kitchen sink

is filled with dirty dishes,"

said Frog.

"Tomorrow," said Toad.

"There is dust on your chairs."

"Tomorrow," said Toad.

"Your windows need scrubbing," said Frog.

"Your plants need watering."

"Tomorrow!" cried Toad.

"I will do it all tomorrow!"

Toad sat on the edge
of his bed.

"Blah," said Toad.

"I feel down in the dumps."

"Why?" asked Frog.

"I am thinking

about tomorrow,"

said Toad.

"I am thinking about

all of the many things

that I will have to do."

"Yes," said Frog,

"tomorrow will be

a very hard day for you."

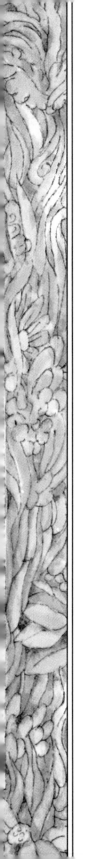

"But Frog," said Toad,

"if I pick up my pants

and jacket right now,

then I will not have to

pick them up tomorrow, will I?"

"No," said Frog.

"You will not have to."

Toad picked up his clothes.

He put them in the closet.

"Frog," said Toad,

"if I wash my dishes right now,

then I will not have to

wash them tomorrow, will I?"

"No," said Frog.

"You will not have to."

Toad washed and dried his dishes.

He put them in the cupboard.

"Frog," said Toad,

"if I dust my chairs

and scrub my windows

and water my plants right now,

then I will not have to

do it tomorrow, will I?"

"No," said Frog. "You will not

have to do any of it."

Toad dusted
his chairs.

He scrubbed
his windows.

He watered
his plants.

"There,"
said Toad.
"Now I feel better.
I am not
in the dumps anymore."
"Why?" asked Frog.
"Because I have done
all that work," said Toad.
"Now I can save tomorrow
for something that I really want to do."
"What is that?" asked Frog.

"Tomorrow," said Toad,

"I can just take life easy."

Toad went back to bed.

He pulled the covers

over his head

and fell asleep.

The Kite

Frog and Toad went out
to fly a kite.
They went to
a large meadow
where the wind was strong.
"Our kite will fly up and up,"
said Frog.
"It will fly all the way up
to the top of the sky."

"Toad," said Frog,

"I will hold the ball of string.

You hold the kite and run."

Toad ran across the meadow.

He ran as fast as his short legs
could carry him.

The kite went up in the air.

It fell to the ground with a bump.

Toad heard laughter.

Three robins were sitting in a bush.

"That kite will not fly,"
said the robins.
"You may as well give up."

Toad ran back to Frog.

"Frog," said Toad,

"this kite will not fly.

I give up."

"We must make a second try,"
said Frog.

"Wave the kite over your head.
Perhaps that will make it fly."

Toad ran back across the meadow.

He waved the kite over his head.

The kite went up in the air
and then fell down with a thud.

"What a joke!" said the robins.

"That kite will never
get off the ground."

Toad ran back to Frog.

"This kite is a joke," he said.

"It will never get off the ground."

"We have to make

a third try," said Frog.

"Wave the kite over your head

and jump up and down.

Perhaps that will make it fly."

Toad ran across

the meadow again.

He waved the kite

over his head.

He jumped up and down.

The kite went up in the air

and crashed down into the grass.

"That kite is junk,"

said the robins.

"Throw it away and go home."

Toad ran back to Frog.

"This kite is junk," he said.

"I think we should

throw it away and go home."

"Toad," said Frog,

"we need one more try.

Wave the kite over your head.

Jump up and down

and shout UP KITE UP."

Toad ran across the meadow.

He waved the kite over his head.

He jumped up and down.

He shouted, "UP KITE UP!"

The kite flew into the air.

It climbed higher and higher.

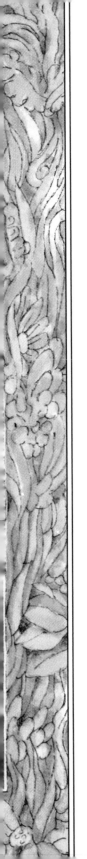

"We did it!" cried Toad.

"Yes," said Frog.

"If a running try

did not work,

and a running and waving try

did not work,

and a running, waving,

and jumping try

did not work,

I knew that

a running, waving, jumping,

and shouting try

just had to work."

The robins flew out of the bush.

But they could not fly

as high as the kite.

Frog and Toad sat

and watched their kite.

It seemed to be flying

way up at the top of the sky.

Shivers

The night was cold and dark.

"Listen to the wind

howling in the trees," said Frog.

"What a fine time for a ghost story."

Toad moved deeper into his chair.

"Toad," asked Frog,

"don't you like to be scared?

Don't you like to feel the shivers?"

"I am not too sure," said Toad.

Frog made a fresh pot of tea.

He sat down

and began a story.

"When I was small," said Frog,

"my mother and father and I

went out for a picnic.

On the way home we lost our way.

My mother was worried.

'We must get home,' she said.

'We do not want to meet

the Old Dark Frog.'

'Who is that?' I asked.

'A terrible ghost,'

said my father.

'He comes out at night and eats

little frog children for supper.'"

Toad sipped his tea.

"Frog," he asked,

"are you making this up?"

"Maybe yes and maybe no,"

said Frog.

"My mother and father
went to search for a path,"
said Frog.
"They told me to wait
until they came back.
I sat under a tree and waited.
The woods became dark.
I was afraid.
Then I saw two huge eyes.
It was the Old Dark Frog.

He was standing near me."

"Frog," asked Toad,

"did this really happen?"

"Maybe it did

and maybe it didn't,"

said Frog.

Frog went on with the story.

"The Dark Frog pulled

a jump rope out of his pocket.

'I am not hungry now,'
said the Dark Frog.
'I have eaten too many
tasty frog children.
But after I jump rope
one hundred times,
I will be hungry again.
Then I will eat YOU!'"

"The Dark Frog tied one end

of the rope to a tree.

'Turn for me!' he shouted.

I turned the rope for the Dark Frog.

He jumped twenty times.

'I am beginning to get hungry,'

said the Dark Frog.

He jumped fifty times.

'I am getting hungrier,'

said the Dark Frog.

He jumped ninety times.

'I am very hungry now!'

said the Dark Frog."

"What happened then?"
asked Toad.

"I had to save my life,"
said Frog.

"I ran around
and around the tree
with the rope.

I tied up
the Old Dark Frog.

He roared and screamed.

I ran away fast."

"I found my mother and father,"
said Frog.

"We came safely home."

"Frog," asked Toad,
"was that a true story?"
"Maybe it was
and maybe it wasn't,"
said Frog.

Frog and Toad sat

close by the fire.

They were scared.

The teacups shook

in their hands.

They were having the shivers.

It was a good, warm feeling.

The Hat

On Toad's birthday

Frog gave him a hat.

Toad was delighted.

"Happy birthday," said Frog.

Toad put on the hat.

It fell down over his eyes.

"I am sorry," said Frog.

"That hat is much too big for you.

I will give you something else."

"No," said Toad. "This hat

is your present to me. I like it.

I will wear it the way it is."

Frog and Toad went for a walk.

Toad tripped over a rock.

He bumped into a tree.

He fell in a hole.

"Frog," said Toad,

"I can't see anything.

I will not be able to wear

your beautiful present.

This is a sad birthday for me."

Frog and Toad

were sad

for a while.

Then Frog said,

"Toad, here is what you must do.

Tonight when you go to bed

you must think

some very big thoughts.

Those big thoughts will make

your head grow larger.

In the morning

your new hat may fit."

"What a good idea," said Toad.

That night when Toad went to bed

he thought the biggest thoughts

that he could think.

Toad thought about

giant sunflowers.

He thought about tall oak trees.

He thought about high mountains

covered with snow.

Then Toad fell asleep.

Frog came into Toad's house.

He came in quietly.

Frog found the hat

and took it to his house.

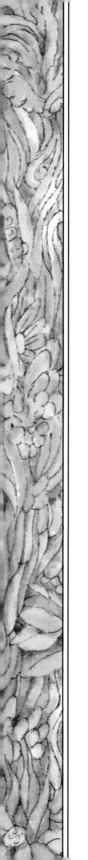

Frog poured some water on the hat.

He put the hat

in a warm place to dry.

It began to shrink.

That hat grew smaller and smaller.

Frog went back to Toad's house.

Toad was still fast asleep.

Frog put the hat back on the hook
where he found it.

When Toad woke up in the morning,
he put the hat on his head.

It was just the right size.

Toad ran to Frog's house.

"Frog, Frog!" he cried.

"All those big thoughts

have made my head

much larger.

Now I can wear your present!"

Frog and Toad went for a walk.

Toad did not trip

over a rock.

He did not bump into a tree.

He did not fall

in a hole.

240

It turned out to be

a very pleasant

day after Toad's birthday.

Alone

Toad went to Frog's house.

He found a note on the door.

The note said,

"Dear Toad, I am not at home.

I went out.

I want to be alone."

"Alone?" said Toad.

"Frog has me for a friend.

Why does he want to be alone?"

Toad looked through the windows.

He looked in the garden.

He did not see Frog.

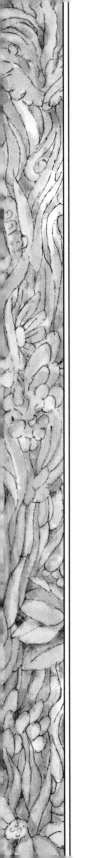

Toad went to the woods.

Frog was not there.

He went to the meadow.

Frog was not there.

Toad went down to the river.

There was Frog.

He was sitting on an island
by himself.

"Poor Frog," said Toad.

"He must be very sad.

I will cheer him up."

Toad ran home.

He made sandwiches.

He made a pitcher of iced tea.

He put everything

in a basket.

Toad hurried

back to the river.

"Frog," he shouted,

"it's me.

It's your best friend, Toad!"

Frog was too far away to hear.

Toad took off his jacket

and waved it like a flag.

Frog was too far away to see.

Toad shouted and waved,

but it was no use.

Frog sat on the island.

He did not see or hear Toad.

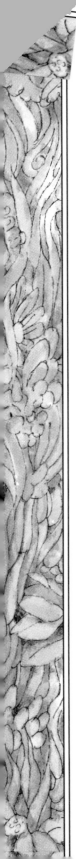

A turtle swam by.

Toad climbed on the turtle's back.

"Turtle," said Toad,

"carry me to the island.

Frog is there.

He wants to be alone."

"If Frog wants to be alone,"

said the turtle,

"why don't you leave him alone?"

"Maybe you are right," said Toad.

"Maybe Frog does not

want to see me.

Maybe he does not want me

to be his friend anymore."

"Yes, maybe," said the turtle

as he swam to the island.

"Frog!" cried Toad.

"I am sorry for all

the dumb things I do.

I am sorry for all

the silly things I say.

Please be my friend again!"

Toad slipped off the turtle.

With a splash, he fell in the river.

Frog pulled Toad

up onto the island.

Toad looked in the basket.

The sandwiches were wet.

The pitcher of iced tea was empty.

"Our lunch is spoiled," said Toad.

"I made it for you, Frog,

so that you would be happy."

"But Toad," said Frog.

"I *am* happy. I am very happy.

This morning

when I woke up

I felt good because

the sun was shining.

I felt good because

I was a frog.

And I felt good because

I have you for a friend.

I wanted to be alone.

I wanted to think about

how fine everything is."

"Oh," said Toad.

"I guess that is a very good reason
for wanting to be alone."

"Now," said Frog,

"I will be glad *not* to be alone.

Let's eat lunch."

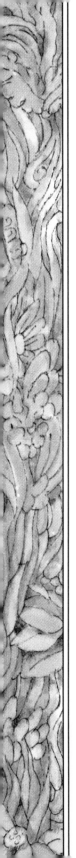

Frog and Toad

stayed on the island

all afternoon.

They ate wet sandwiches

without iced tea.

They were two close friends

sitting alone together.